The Snow Thing

Story retold by Gill Howell
Pictures by Helen Cann

OXFORD
UNIVERSITY PRESS

Once, long ago in winter, in a cold, cold land there lived a poor man and his two daughters. Their home was a small wooden house near the forest, far away from the towns and cities.

Katya, the younger daughter, was happy to work in the house, cleaning and cooking for her father and sister. But Ivanka, the elder daughter, was not satisfied. She wished for a rich husband, servants, and a castle to live in. And although the poor man went out every day to find work, there was little work to be found. It was hard to earn enough to buy food.

Ivanka was a great beauty and her father longed to dress her in rich furs and beaded cloaks. But Ivanka's heart was as cold as ice. She sat by the fire, dreaming of riches. Katya, the younger daughter, did all the housework.

One day the snow fell and fell. It lay on the
ground and on the roof, thick and heavy.

"Father," said Katya. "Won't you stay in today
and keep warm?"

"And then what would we do for food?" cried
Ivanka.

"Keep the fire burning until I return," called
the poor man, as once more he went out to
find work.

When their father had gone, Katya went out into the snow to collect wood, but Ivanka just sat by the fire.

Katya cleaned the little house, and prepared the food for when their father came home, but Ivanka just sat by the fire.

All day she sat and dreamed, while Katya cleaned and washed and cooked.

But then a great storm came. The wind blew the snow through the cracks in the wooden walls and through gaps in the windows. It blew snow under the door and across the floor.

All day, as the snow settled around
her, Ivanka sat dreaming by the fire.
And then the wind blew ice and snow
down the chimney. The fire spluttered
and went out. The house quickly grew cold
and dark.

At last Ivanka wrapped a warm shawl
around her and left the cold fireside.

"Katya!" cried Ivanka. "Fetch more wood.
Quickly! You must get the fire burning again,
before Father returns."

So Katya wrapped her old grey cloak around her, opened the door and struggled out into the deep snow.

The cold wind blew. Snow soaked through her cloak as Katya gathered wood among the trees of the forest.

Deep snow had blown over the ground under the trees. Soon Katya's hands were frozen, for she had no gloves to wear. Soon Katya's feet felt like lumps of ice, for the snow soaked through her thin boots.

Suddenly, a strange old man in thin rags came up to her. His face was wrinkled, but his bright blue eyes were kind. Katya did not feel afraid.

"Child," he said, "will you spare a little wood, for I cannot bend to pick up my own?"

"Here, Grandfather," smiled Katya, giving all her wood to him. "Take this bundle and have a good fire to warm you."

Katya turned away and began to gather wood again. Her feet were so very cold she could barely walk. Her hands were so very cold, that she could only collect a small bundle before returning home.

As she made her way home, there, at the edge of the forest, she saw a great bonfire. No snow lay near the fire, and a huge man dressed in a red and gold cloak trimmed with fur stood beside it. In his wrinkled face shone a pair of bright blue eyes.

"Katya," he called to her, "I am the Snow King. Do not fear. Come close to the fire and sit. Warm yourself, child. Warm your hands and feet, then eat, and rest."

A table appeared beside the fire, spread with every kind of delicious food she had ever seen. And so Katya sat close by the fire and ate. Soon she felt warm and full of good food. As she thanked the Snow King for his kindness, her eyelids grew heavy and she fell into a deep sleep.

When she awoke it was dark. The fire and the Snow King were gone. But Katya was warmly dressed all in a red and gold fur cloak, and soft fur boots were on her feet. Straight away, Katya picked up her bundle of wood and ran through the snow to her father's house.

Katya's father was happy to see her safe, but Ivanka cried in anger when she saw her sister.

"I sat in a cold dark house while you warmed yourself by a fire!" she shouted.

"Go into the forest, Ivanka," cried the poor man when he heard Katya's story. "You too must meet the Snow King. You are so beautiful. He is sure to give you even more riches."

So Ivanka wrapped her old grey cloak around her and went out into the snow. She only gathered a little wood, and spent her time looking about for the Snow King.

Soon Ivanka met a poor old man in thin rags. His face was wrinkled but his eyes were blue and bright.

"Child," he said, "will you spare a little wood for I cannot bend to pick up my own."

"Be gone!" she shouted. "I am waiting for the Snow King, not an old beggar!"

Suddenly the old man threw off his rags and there stood the Snow King, dressed in a red and gold fur cloak. His bright blue eyes flashed in anger.

"Your heart is ice," cried the Snow King, "and you shall be too!"

Ivanka's nose turned into an icicle. She froze to the spot. And there she stood in the deep snow of the forest. She saw the snow falling and felt the cold frost on her skin.

And there she stayed all winter until the first warmth of spring melted her heart.